When I Grow Up

Written and illustrated by

P.K. Hallinan

*For Sara Anderson,
the kind of person I want to be
when I grow up.*

Ideals Children's Books • Nashville, Tennessee

Published by Ideals Children's Books
An imprint of Hambleton-Hill Publishing, Inc.
Nashville, Tennessee 37218

Printed and bound in the United States of America

Library of Congress Cataloging-in-Publication Data

Hallinan, P.K.
        When I grow up / by P.K. Hallinan.
            p.   cm.
        Summary: A child ponders possible occupations from A (for actor) to Z
    (for zookeeper).
        ISBN 1-57102-061-6 (lib. bdg.)—ISBN 1-57102-046-2 (paper)
        [1. Occupations—Fiction. 2. Alphabet. 3. Stories in rhyme.] I. Title.
    PZ8.3.H15Wq   1995
    [E]—dc20   95-8293
                                                                  CIP
                                                                   AC

When I grow up,
I know I can be
whatever I dream of,
from **A** down to **Z**.

I might be an **A**ctor,

the star of the show,

and quote William Shakespeare

wherever I go.

Or I might be a **B**aker
whose favorite treat
is baking up biscuits
with flour and wheat!

There's really no end

to the things I can do:

I could be a **C**arpenter . . .

and a Tap **D**ancer too!

An **E**ngineer, **F**ireman,

or **G**olfer is fine . . .

so is a **H**omemaker—

I'll have a great time!

or a **Jockey** on horseback—
now, *that* would be nice!

I could be a **K**icker

who brings a team glory . . .

or a lively **L**ibrarian

who likes to share stories.

Yes, when I grow up,
I am certain to find
my tasks can be mastered
with patience and time.

I'll be a **M**usician
or maybe a **N**urse—
or an **O**pera star singing
an aria verse.

A **P**oliceman on wheels

or a **Q**uiz Show MC

or a **R**adio DJ—

they're all fine with me!

Even a **S**cientist
might be the one
or a wonderful **T**eacher
who makes learning fun!

Yes, when I grow up,
I am certain to learn
that enjoyment means more
than the money I'll earn.

I could be an **U**mpire,
a **V**eterinarian, or **W**aiter;
a **X**ylophone player—
and what could be greater?

But I might want to be
a **Y**odeler supreme
or a happy **Z**ookeeper—
now, *that's* a great dream!

For whatever I do,

from **A** down to **Z**,

I'm bound to succeed

if I stay true to *me*.

So I'll reach for the stars

to fill up my cup,

but I'll choose from my heart . . .